The Malady of Death

OTHER WORKS BY MARGUERITE DURAS

Published by Grove Press

India Song

Four Novels: The Square;
    10:30 on a Summer Night;
    The Afternoon of Mr. Andesmas;
    Moderato Cantabile

Hiroshima Mon Amour

The Malady of Death

by
MARGUERITE DURAS

translated from the French
by Barbara Bray

GROVE PRESS, INC., NEW YORK

First published in 1982 by
Les Editions de Minuit, Paris
First Grove Press Edition 1986
First Printing 1986
ISBN: 0-394-53866-8
Library of Congress Catalog Card Number: 83-49427

First Evergreen Edition 1986
First Printing 1986
ISBN: 0-394-62175-1
Library of Congress Catalog Card Number: 83-49427

Library of Congress Cataloging in Publication Data

Duras, Marguerite.
    The malady of death.

    Translation of: La maladie de la morte.
    1. Duras, Marguerite—Translations, English.
I. Title.
PQ2607.U8245A2   1986   843'.912   83-49427
ISBN 0-394-53866-8

Book design by Hannah Lerner

Printed in the United States of America

Grove Press, Inc., 196 West Houston Street
New York, N.Y. 10014

5   4   3   2   1

You wouldn't have known her, you'd have seen her everywhere at once, in a hotel, in a street, in a train, in a bar, in a book, in a film, in yourself, your inmost self, when your sex grew erect in the night, seeking somewhere to put itself, somewhere to shed its load of tears.

I

*

You may have paid her.

May have said: I want you to come every night for a few days.

She'd have given you a long look and said in that case it'd be expensive.

And then she says: What is it you want?

You say you want to try, try it, try to know, to get used to that body, those breasts, that scent. To beauty, to the risk of having children implicit in that body, to that hairless unmuscular body, that face, that naked skin, to the identity between that skin and the life it contains.
2

You say you want to try, for several days perhaps.

Perhaps for several weeks.

Perhaps even for your whole life.

Try what? she asks.

Loving, you answer.

She asks: Yes, but why?

You say so as to sleep with your sex at rest, somewhere unknown.

You say you want to try, to weep there, in that particular place.

She smiles and says: Do you want me, too?

You say: Yes. I don't know

that yet and I want to penetrate there too, and with my usual force. They say it offers more resistance, it's smooth but it offers more resistance than emptiness does.

She says she has no opinion on the subject. How should she know?

She asks: What other conditions?

You say she mustn't speak, like the women of her ancestors, must yield completely to you and to your will, be entirely submissive like peasant women

4

in the barns after the harvest when they're exhausted and let the men come to them while they're asleep. So that you may gradually get used to that shape molding itself to yours, at your mercy as nuns are at God's. And also so that little by little, as day dawns, you may be less afraid of not knowing where to put your body or at what emptiness to aim your love.

She looks at you. Then stops looking at you and looks at something else. Then answers.

She says in that case it'll be even more expensive. She tells you how much.

You accept.

Every day she'd come. Every day she comes.

The first day she strips and lies down where you tell her to on the bed.

You watch her go to sleep. She doesn't speak. Just goes to sleep. All night you watch her.

She'd come at night. She comes at night.

All night you watch her. For two nights you watch her.

For two nights she scarcely speaks.
6

Then one night she does. She speaks.

She asks if she's managing to make your body less lonely. You say you can't really understand the word as applied to you. That you can't distinguish between thinking you're lonely and actually becoming lonely. As with you, you add.

And then once in the middle of the night she asks: What time of year is it?

You say: Not yet winter. Autumn still.

And she asks: What's that sound?

You say: The sea.

She asks: Where?

You say: There beyond that wall.

She goes back to sleep.

Young. She'd be young. In her clothes and hair there'd be a clinging smell, you'd try to identify it, and in the end your experience would enable you to do so. You'd say: A smell of heliotrope and citron. She answers: Whatever you say.

One evening you do it, as arranged, you sleep with your face between her parted legs, up

8

against her sex, already in the moistness of her body, where she opens. She offers no resistance.

Another evening you inadvertently give her pleasure and she cries out.

You tell her not to. She says she won't anymore.

She doesn't.

No woman will ever cry out because of you now.

Perhaps you get from her a

pleasure you've never known before. I don't know. Nor do I know if you hear the low, distant murmur of her pleasure through her breathing, through the faint rattle going back and forth between her mouth and the outside air. I don't think so.

She opens her eyes and says: What joy.

You put your hand over her mouth to silence her. Tell her one doesn't say such things.

She shuts her eyes.

Says she won't say it again.

She asks if *they* talk about it. You say no.

She asks what they do talk

about. You say they talk about everything else. Everything except that.

She laughs and goes back to sleep.

Sometimes you pace the room, around the bed or along the walls by the sea.

Sometimes you weep.

Sometimes you go out on the terrace in the growing cold.

You don't know what's in the sleep of the girl on the bed.

You'd like to start from that body and get back to the bodies of others, to your own, to get

back to yourself. And yet it's because you must do this that you
weep.

And she, in the room, sleeps
on. Sleeps, and you don't wake
her. As her sleep goes on, sor-
row grows in the room. You
sleep, once, on the floor at the
foot of her bed.

She goes on sleeping, evenly.
So deeply, she sometimes smiles.
She wakes only if you touch her
body, the breasts, the eyes.
Sometimes she wakes for no rea-
son, except to ask if the noise is
the wind or high tide.

She wakes. She looks at you. She says: The malady's getting more and more of a hold on you. It's reached your eyes, your voice.

You ask: What malady?

She says she can't say, yet.

Night after night you enter the dark of her sex, almost unwittingly take that blind way. Sometimes you stay there; sleep there, inside her, all night long, so as to be ready if ever, through some involuntary movement on her part or yours, you should feel like taking her again, filling her again, taking pleasure in her again. But only with a pleasure, as always, blinded by tears.

She'd always be ready, willing or no. That's just what you'll never know. She's more mysterious than any other external thing you've ever known.
Nor will you, or anyone else, ever know how she sees, how she thinks, either of the world or of you, of your body or your mind, or of the malady she says you suffer from. She doesn't know, herself. She couldn't tell you. You couldn't find out anything about it from her.

You'd never know anything, neither you nor anyone else, about what she thinks of you or of this affair. However many ages may bury both your forgotten existences, no one will ever know. She is incapable of knowing.

Because you know nothing about her you'd say she knows nothing about you. You'd leave it at that.

She'd have been tall. With a long body made in a single sweep, at a single stroke, as if

15

by God Himself, with the un-
alterable perfection of individ-
uality.

For she'd have been unlike
anyone else.

The body's completely de-
fenseless, smooth from face to
feet. It invites strangulation,
rape, ill usage, insult, shouts of
hatred, the unleashing of deadly
and unmitigated passions.

You look at her.

She's very slim, almost frail.
Her legs have a beauty distinct
from that of the body. They
don't really belong to the rest of
the body.

You say: You must be very
beautiful.

16

She says: I'm here right in front of you. Look for yourself.

You say: I can't see anything.

She says: Try. It's all part of the bargain.

You take hold of the body and look at its different areas. You turn it round, keep turning it round. Look at it, keep looking at it.

Then you give up.

Give up. Stop touching it.

Until that night you hadn't realized how ignorant one might be of what the eyes see, the hands and the body touch. Now you find out.

You say: I can't see anything.
She doesn't answer.
She's asleep.

You wake her up. Ask her if she's a prostitute. She shakes her head.

You ask her why she accepted the deal and the paid nights.

She answers in a voice still drowsy, almost inaudible: Because as soon as you spoke to me I saw you were suffering from the malady of death. For the first few days I couldn't put a name to it. Then I could.

You ask her to say the words

again. She does. Repeats them: The malady of death.

You ask her how she knows. She says she just does. Says one knows without knowing how.

You ask: Why is the malady of death fatal? She answers: Because whoever has it doesn't know he's a carrier, of death. And also because he's like to die without any life to die to, and without even knowing that's what he's doing.

Her eyes are still closed. It's as if she were resting from an immemorial weariness. While

19

she sleeps you've forgotten the color of her eyes, as you have the name you called her by the first evening. Then you realize it's not the color of her eyes that will always be an insurmountable barrier between you and her. No, not the color—you know that would be somewhere between green and gray. Not the color, no. The look.

The look.

You realize she's looking at you.

You cry out. She turns to the wall.

She says: It's going to end, don't worry.

*

With one arm you lift her and hold her up against you, she's so light. You look.

Strangely, her breasts are brown, the areolas almost black. You eat them, drink them, and nothing in her body flinches, she offers no resistance, none. Perhaps at one point you cry out again. Another time you tell her to say a word, just one, the one that's your name, you tell her what it is. She doesn't answer, and you cry out again. And it's then she smiles. And it's then you know she's alive.

21

The smile vanishes. She hasn't said the name.

You go on looking. Her face is given over to sleep, it's silent, asleep, like her hands. But all the time the spirit shows through the surface of the body, all over, so that each part bears witness in itself to the whole— the hand and the eyes, the curve of the belly and the face, the breasts and the sex, the legs and the arms, the breath, the heart, the temples, the temples and time.

You go out again onto the terrace facing the black sea.

Inside you there are sobs you can't explain. They linger on the brink of you as if they were outside, they can't reach you and be wept. Facing the black sea, leaning against the wall of the room where she's sleeping, you weep for yourself as a stranger might.

You go back into the room. She's asleep. You don't understand. She's sleeping, naked, there on the bed. You can't understand how it's possible for her not to know of your tears, for her to be protected from you by herself, for her to be so completely unaware of how she fills the whole world.

You lie down beside her. And, still for yourself, you weep.

Then it's almost dawn. Then there's a dark light in the room, of indeterminate hue. Then you switch some lights on, to see her. Her. See what you've never seen before, the hidden sex, that which swallows up and holds without seeming to. See it like this, closed up around its own sleep. And also to see the freckles strewn all over her from the hairline right down to where the breasts begin, where they give under their own weight, hooked onto the hinge of the arms, and right up to the closed lids and the pale half-open lips. You think: They're in the places of the summer sun, the open places, the places on view.

She sleeps.

You switch the lights off.

It's almost light.

It's still almost dawn. These hours are as vast as stretches of sky. It's too much, time can't find a way through. Time has stopped passing. You tell yourself it would be best for her to die. You tell yourself that if now, at this hour of the night, she died, it would be easier. For you, you probably mean, but you don't finish the sentence.

You listen to the sound of the tide starting to rise. The stranger is there on the bed, in the white expanse of white sheets. The whiteness makes her shape look darker, more present than an animal presence suddenly deserted by life, more present than the presence of death.

You look at this shape, and as

you do so you realize its infernal power, its abominable frailty, its weakness, the unconquerable strength of its incomparable weakness.

You go out of the room, go out again onto the terrace facing the sea, away from her smell.

A fine drizzle is falling, the sea is still black under a sky bleached of light. You can hear it. The black water goes on rising, gets nearer, moving, always moving. Long white rollers run across it, a long swell that crashes in a turmoil of white.

The black sea is a heavy one. There's a storm in the offing, as there often is at night. You stand for a long while, watching.

It occurs to you that the black sea is moving in the stead of something else, of you and of the dark shape on the bed.

You finish your sentence. You tell yourself that if now, at this hour of the night, she died, it would be easier for you to make her disappear off the face of the earth, to throw her into the black water, it would only take a few minutes to throw a body as light as that into the rising tide, and free the bed of the stench of heliotrope and citron.

*

Back into the room you go
again. She is there, sleeping,
abandoned in her own darkness,
her magnificence.

You realize she's so made that
it's as if at any moment, at her
own whim, her body could cease
to live, could just thin out
around her and disappear from
sight, and that it's in this threat
that she sleeps, exposes herself
to your view. That it's in the risk
she runs, with the sea so close
and empty and black still, that
she sleeps.

*

Around the body, the room. Probably your room. But it's inhabited by her, a woman. You can't recognize it anymore. It's emptied of life, without either you or your like. Occupied only by the long, lithe streak of the alien form on the bed.

She stirs, her eyes half open. She asks: How many paid nights left? You say: Three.

She asks: Haven't you ever loved a woman? You say no, never.

She asks: Haven't you ever desired a woman? You say no, never.

She asks: Not once, not for a single moment? You say no, never.

She says: Never? Ever? You repeat: Never.

She smiles, says: A dead man's a strange thing.

She goes on: What about looking, haven't you ever looked at a woman? You say no, never.

She asks: What do you look at? You say: Everything else.

She stretches, is silent. Smiles. Goes back to sleep.

You come back into the room. She hasn't moved in the white expanse of the sheets. You look at her whom you've never approached, ever, either through others like her or through herself.

You look at the shape suspected through the ages. You give up.

You stop looking. Stop looking at anything. You shut your eyes so as to get back into your difference, your death.

When you open your eyes she's still there. Still there.

You go back towards the alien body. It's sleeping.

You look at the malady of your life, the malady of death. It's on

32

her, on her sleeping body, that you look at it. You look at the different places on the body, at the face, the breasts, the mingled site of the sex.

You look at where the heart is. The beat seems different, more distant. The word occurs to you: more alien. It's regular, it seems as if it would never stop. You bring your body close to the object that is her body. It's warm, moist. She's still alive. While she lives she invites murder. You wonder how to kill her and who will. You don't love anything or anyone, you don't even love the difference you think you embody. All you know is the grace of the bodies of the dead, the grace of those like yourself. Suddenly you see the difference between the grace of the bodies of the dead and this grace here, this royalty, made of utmost weakness, which could be crushed by the merest gesture.

You realize it's here, in her, that the malady of death is fomenting, that it's this shape stretched out before you that decrees the malady of death.

*

Out of the half-open mouth comes a breath that returns, withdraws, returns again. The fleshly machine is marvelously precise. Leaning over her, motionless, you look at her. You know you can dispose of her in whatever way you wish, even the most dangerous. But you don't. Instead you stroke her body as gently as if it ran the risk of happiness. Your hand is over the sex, between the open lips, it's there it strokes. You look at the opening and what surrounds it, the whole body. You don't see anything.

You want to see all of a woman, as much as possible. You don't see that for you it's impossible.

You look at the closed shape.

First you see slight tremors showing on the skin, just like those of suffering. And then you see the eyelids flicker as if the eyes wanted to see. And then you see the mouth open as if it wanted to say something. And then you notice that under your caresses the lips of her sex are swelling up, and that from their smoothness comes a hot sticky liquid, as it might be blood. Then you stroke more quickly.

And you see that her thighs are opening to give your hand more room, so that you can stroke better than before.

And suddenly, in a moan, you see pleasure come upon her, take possession of her, make her arch up from the bed. You look intently at what you have just done to her body. Then you see it fall back inert on the white of the bed. It breathes fast, in gasps that get further and further apart. And then the eyes shut tighter than before, sink deeper into the face. Then they open,

37

and then they shut again.

They shut.

You've looked at everything. At last you too shut your eyes. You stay like that a long time, with your eyes shut, like her.

You think of outside your room, of the streets in the town, the lonely little squares over by the station. Of those winter Saturdays all alike.

And then you listen to the approaching sound. To the sea.

*

You listen to the sea. It's very close to the walls of the room. Through the windows that colorless light still, the slowness of the day to spread over the sky, the black sea still, the sleeping body, the stranger in the room.

And then you do it. I couldn't say why. I see you do it without knowing why. You could go out of the room and leave the body, the sleeping form. But no, you do it, apparently as another would, but with the complete difference that separates you from her. You do it, you go back towards the body.

You cover it completely with your own, you draw it towards

you so as not to crush it with your strength, so as not to kill it, and then you do it, you return to the nightly dwelling, you are engulfed.

You stay on in that abode. You go on weeping. You think you know you know not what, you can't go through with that knowledge, you think you alone are the image of the world's woe, of a special fate. You think you're the master of the event now taking place, you think it exists.

She sleeps, a smile on her lips, fit to be killed.

You stay on in the abode of her body.

40

She is full of you as she sleeps. The faintly voiced tremors that go through the body become more and more marked. She's in a dream of happiness at being full of a man, of you, or of someone else, or of someone else again.

You weep.

The tears wake her. She looks at you. She looks at the room. And again at you. She strokes your hand. Asks: Why are you crying? You say it's for her to say, she's the one who ought to know.

41

She answers softly, gently: Because you don't love. You say that's it.

She asks you to say it clearly. You say: I don't love.

She says: Never?

You say: Never.

She says: The wish to be about to kill a lover, to keep him for yourself, yourself alone, to take him, steal him in defiance of every law, every moral authority—you don't know what that is, you've never experienced it?

You say: Never.

She looks at you, repeats: A dead man's a strange thing.

*

She asks if you've seen the sea,
asks if it's day, if it's light.

You say the sun's rising, but
that at this time of year it takes
a long time to light up the whole
sky.

She asks you what color the
sea is.

You say: Black.

She says the sea's never black.
You must be mistaken.

You ask if she thinks anyone
could love you.

She says no, not possibly. You

43

ask: Because of the death? She
says: Yes, because your feelings
are so dull and sluggish, because you lied and said the sea
is black.

And then she is silent.

You're afraid she'll go to sleep
again, you rouse her and say: Go
on talking. She says: Ask ques-
tions then, I can't do it on my
own. Again you ask if anyone
could love you. Again she says:
No.

She says that a moment ago
you wanted to kill her, when you
came in off the terrace and into
the room for the second time.
That she knew this in her sleep,
44

from the way you looked at her. She asks you to say why.

You say you can't know why, that you don't understand the malady you suffer from.

She smiles, says this is the first time, that until she met you she didn't know death could be lived.

She looks at you through the filtered green of her eyes. She says: You herald the reign of death. Death can't be loved if it's imposed from outside. You think you weep because you can't love. You weep because you can't impose death.

She's already almost asleep. She says almost inaudibly: You're going to die of death. Your death has already begun.

You weep. She says: Don't cry, it's pointless, give up the habit of weeping for yourself, it's pointless.

Imperceptibly the room is filled with the still dark light of the sun.

She opens her eyes, shuts them again. She says: Two more

paid nights and it will be over. She smiles and strokes your eyes. She smiles ironically in her sleep.

You go on talking, all alone in the world, just as you wish. You say love has always struck you as out of place, you've never understood, you've always avoided loving, always wanted to be free not to. You say you're lost. But that you don't know what you're lost to. Or in.

She's not listening, she's asleep.

You tell a story about a child.

The light has reached the windows.

She opens her eyes, says: Stop lying. She says she hopes she'll never know anything, anything in the world, the way you do. She says: I don't want to know anything the way you do, with that death-derived certainty, that hopeless monotony, the same every day of your life, every night, and that deadly routine of lovelessness.

She says: It's day, everything is about to begin, except you, you never begin.

She goes back to sleep. You ask her why she sleeps, what weariness she has to rest from, what monumental weariness.

48

She lifts her hand and strokes your face again, the mouth perhaps. She smiles ironically again in her sleep. She says: The fact that you ask the question proves you can't understand. She says it's a way of resting from you too. From death.

You go on with the story about the child, cry it out aloud. You say you don't know the whole of the story about him, about you. You say you've been told it. She smiles, says she's heard and read it too, often, everywhere, in a number of books. You ask how loving can happen—the emotion of loving.

She answers: Perhaps a sudden lapse in the logic of the universe. She says: Through a mistake, for instance. She says: Never through an act of will. You ask: Could the emotion of loving come from other things too? You beg her to say. She says: It can come from anything, from the flight of a night bird, from a sleep, from a dream of sleep, from the approach of death, from a word, from a crime, of itself, from oneself, often without knowing how. She says: Look. She parts her legs, and in the hollow between you see the dark night at last. You say: It

50

was there, the dark night. It's there.

She says: Come. You do. Having entered her, you go on weeping. She says: Don't cry anymore. She says: Take me, so it may have been done.

You do so, you take her.

It is done.

She goes back to sleep.

One day she isn't there anymore. You wake and she isn't there. She has gone during the night. The mark of her body is still there on the sheets. Cold.

It's dawn today. The sun's not

yet up, but the edges of the sky are already light, while from its center a thick darkness still falls on the earth.

There's nothing left in the room but you. Her body has vanished. The difference between her and you is confirmed by her sudden absence.

Far away, on the beaches, gulls would be crying in the last of the dark, already starting to feed on the lugworms, to scour the sand abandoned by the receding tide. In the dark, the crazy din of the ravenous gulls— it's suddenly as if you'd never heard it before.

*

She'd never come back.

The evening after she goes, you tell the story of the affair in a bar. At first you tell it as if it were possible to do so, then you give up. Then you tell it laughing, as if it were impossible for it to have happened or possible for you to have invented it.

The next day, suddenly, perhaps you'd notice her absence in the room. The next day, you'd perhaps feel a desire to see her there again, in the strangeness of your solitude, as a stranger herself.

Perhaps you'd look for her outside your room, on the beaches, outside cafés, in the streets. But you wouldn't be able to find her, because in the light of day you can't recognize anyone. You wouldn't recognize her. All you know of her is her sleeping body beneath her shut or half-shut eyes. The penetration of one body by another—that you can't recognize, ever. You couldn't ever.

When you wept it was just over yourself and not because of the marvelous impossibility of reaching her through the difference that separates you.

54

*

All you remember of the whole affair are certain words she said in her sleep, the ones that tell you what's wrong with you: the malady of death.

Soon you give up, don't look for her anymore, either in the town or at night or in the daytime.

Even so you have managed to live that love in the only way possible for you. Losing it before it happened.

The Malady of Death could be staged in the theatre.

The young woman of the paid nights should be lying on some white sheets in the middle of the stage. She might be naked. A man would walk back and forth around her, telling the story.

Only the woman would speak her lines from memory. The man never would. He would read the text, either standing still or walking about around the young woman.

56

The man the story is about would never appear. Even when he speaks to the young woman he does so only through the man who reads his story.

Acting is replaced here by reading. I always think nothing can replace the reading of a text, that no acting can ever equal the effect of a text not memorised.

So the two actors should speak as if they were reading the text in separate rooms, isolated from one another.

The text would be completely nullified if it were spoken theatrically.

The man's voice should be rather high-pitched, the woman's deep and almost off-hand.

The man's pacings to and fro around the young woman's body should be long-drawn-out. He ought to disappear from view, to be lost in the theatre just as he is lost in time, and then to return into the light, to us.

The stage should be low, almost at floor level, so that the young woman's body is completely visible to the audience.

There should be great stretches of silence between the different paid nights, silences in which nothing happens except the passage of time.

58

The man reading the text should seem to be suffering from a fundamental and fatal weakness—the same as that of the other, the man we don't see.

The young woman should be beautiful, distinctive.

A big dark opening admits the sound of the sea—always the same black rectangle, never any lighter. But the sound of the sea does vary in volume.

The young woman's departure isn't seen. There should be a blackout when she disappears, and when the light comes up again there is nothing left but the white sheets in the middle of the stage and the sound of the sea surging in through the black door.

No music.

If I ever filmed this text I'd want the weeping by the sea to be shot in such a way that the white turmoil of the waves is seen almost simultaneously with the man's face. There should be a correlation between the white of the sheets and the white of the sea. The sheets should be a prior image of the sea.

All this by way of general suggestion.